The Squeaky Adventures of Dora

by

Olivia Tartan

Let me introduce you to a dog named Dora

Dora is tall, Dora is sleek, Dora is friendly and she likes to sneak. Dora likes cuddles and Dora likes treats, Dora thinks it's neat to steal the things that go on your feet!

But one thing you should know, she moves with a beat which is more like a SQUEAK!

Dora wants your company so she can show you her individuality, so let's continue to the next quest, while she gives us another test.

The morning birds tweet with those things called their beaks and Dora rises ready to eat. Before she can eat, she sneaks and grabs a peek before she steals those things that go on your FEET.

Her Master who is no longer asleep chases Dora who leaps into a beat forgetting to keep the place all neat, just wishing she can now EAT.

Just as Dora's breakfast is being prepared, she sits down looking very petite and all of a sudden she lets out one loud SQUEAK.

Dora's breakfast bowl is placed in position waiting for her
Master to beep out the words "go eat" but not before
Dora lets out one more excited SQUEAK.

Dora favours many flavours and she loves all types of eatables, even all sorts of meat and vegetables. She tucks into some pumpkin, a carrot, an apple or two, and is now craving a banana or few.

The list can go on but we cannot forget her love for something smelling fishy cause she thinks they're nice and squishy. Dora fancies sardines and eating them are part of her routine.

She gives praise to her Master by wiping that fishy mouth all over her blouse. Dora's healthy diet is a necessity for her longevity because we want to spend more time with our best friend, all the way to the end.

Dora is bright, Dora is smart, Dora is nice but just some words of advice, she might need a lesson or two or she might be teaching you a few. She must behave and must know what is wrong and what is right otherwise this one is going to have quite a FRIGHT.

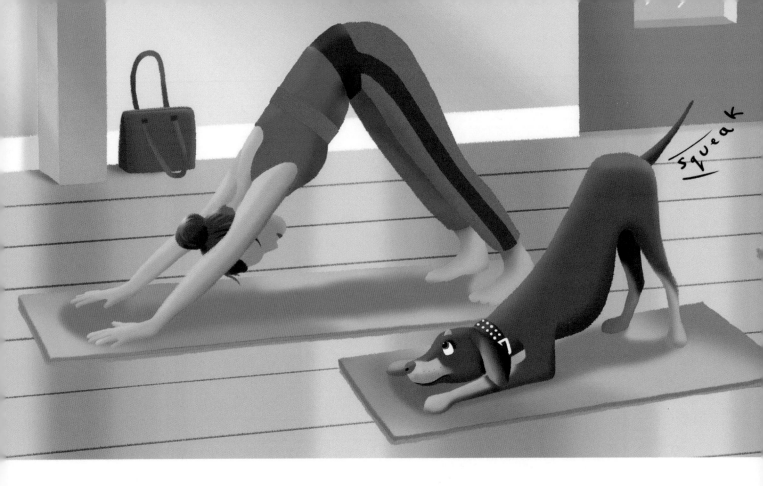

In the morning and we're off the sofa where Dora joins her Master to do her yoga. Together we start then we park ourselves apart. We strengthen the back and something that was once called a six pack. Dora likes to show off her physique thinking she's all that mystique and now here come some SQUEAKS, so she can feel complete.

Off to the park so that Dora doesn't bark. She needs to get out so she can stay fit throughout. Dora lets out a waggle cause she likes dogs that are all different breeds, shapes and sizes. When Dora finally arrives to the park, she circles like a shark. She keeps her four-legged friends in check and gets ready to connect.

Dora's three-legged friend Hazel who gets all of our praises is more than just able and is here to be playful. Hazel is quick on her paws even though she doesn't have all fours. There is only one dog that can steal a ball back and it's Hazel from the tail pack.

When it's time to leave the park, Dora doesn't want to depart, she runs away hoping she can have one more play. When Dora is finally restrained, she still complains wishing she could be unchained. Although she wants to stay, she thinks about the next meet and remembers it's time to EAT.

Back at home, Dora is hanging about with her mind scanning throughout which can only mean she is keen to be the cheeky machine. Dora creeps and then she sneaks. She finds her Master speaking with some peeps.

Dora sneaks some more but this time with technique.
Dora comes by her Master then lets out one loud SQUEAK,
now nobody can speak. Dora is now complete so she can
sneak back into her retreat.

After all that work, Dora wants something to eat so she lets out a SQUEAK just as if she could speak. Dora drools down into a pool at your feet, looking at you lovingly asking for her treat. Dora lets out one more SQUEAK just to continue the beat and lets you know she's ready to EAT.

Dora is a guard dog too and sometimes needs back up with a few. One by one she takes her toy dogs outside. They guard the family yard as if they thought they were Scotland yard. Dora's toy dogs even takes her shift cause Dora has her needs and proceeds like her breed, about to catch up on some Zzzz's.

When its nap time, there's no exact TIME but Dora will say for the last time she needs a cozy bed TIME. It doesn't take long for Dora to fall into a trance, not long her legs let out a dance.

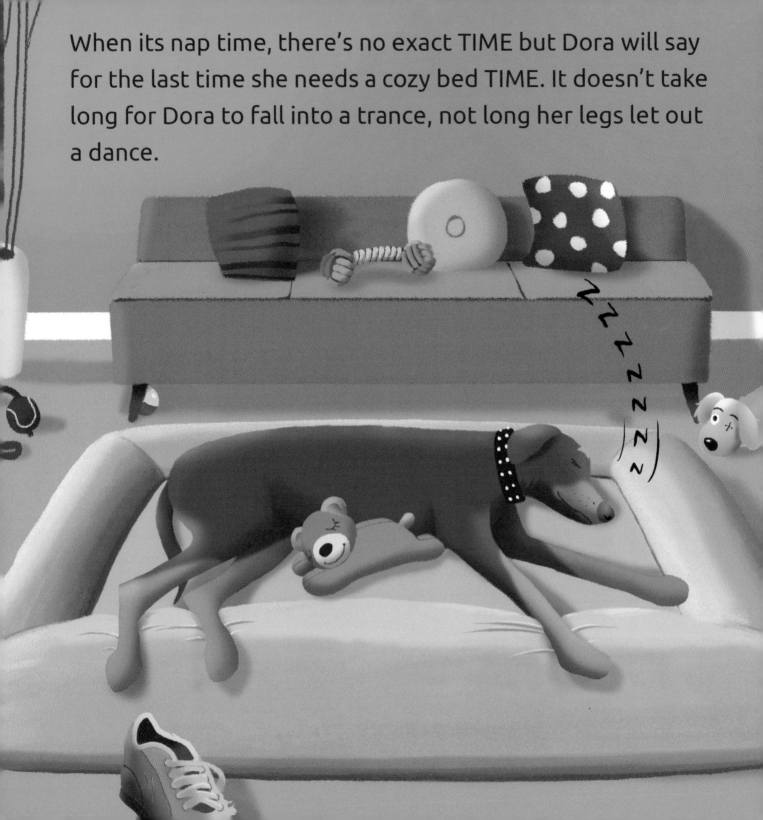

squeak

Dora is always ready to eat and can't wait to sneak
a peek and maybe have some dinner to eat because
nothing beats her favourite vegetables with some other
delectables. Dora MUNCHES and SLURPS then lets out a
BURP. MUNCHES and CRUNCHES because she misses out
on all your lunches. Patiently waiting, what else can she
do? There's nothing else left for her to do but to let out a
SQUEAK.

At the end of the day, Dora loves to cuddle and huddles into your lap. She says thank you for spending time with you by asking to have a pat or two. She even loved the food her Master gave and gives praise for all the games she played. Dora brings you her favourite toy with so much joy to show how much she loves you so let's enjoy.

Whenever we have been apart, we always know how to restart even if it means Dora lets out a fart. Our bond has so much humour and I wish I met you so much sooner.

About the Author

Olivia Tartan is a newly published author of children's books based in Brisbane, Australia.
Passionate about animals and her adoring dog Dora, Olivia is always learning healthy recipes to cook for her dog and enjoys getting outdoors socialising Dora.

Printed in Great Britain
by Amazon

36930427R00018